# GRANNY
## CAME HERE
## ON THE
# EMPIRE
# WINDRUSH

To those that come from across the world,
I hope you find love and peace – P.L.

To my very own grandparents from Trinidad and St. Lucia,
Melita Sucre and Felicity Hypolite – C.S.

First published 2022 by Nosy Crow Ltd
The Crow's Nest, 14 Baden Place, Crosby Row, London, SE1 1YW, UK
Nosy Crow Eireann Ltd, 44 Orchard Grove, Kenmare, Co Kerry, V93 FY22, Ireland
www.nosycrow.com

ISBN 978 1 78800 814 3 (HB)
ISBN 978 1 83994 231 0 (PB)

Nosy Crow and associated logos are trademarks and/or registered trademarks
of Nosy Crow Ltd

Text © Patrice Lawrence 2022
Illustrations © Camilla Sucre 2022

The right of Patrice Lawrence to be identified as the author of this work and of
Camilla Sucre to be identified as the illustrator of this work has been asserted.

A CIP catalogue record for this book is available from the British Library.

Printed in Italy.
Papers used by Nosy Crow are made from wood grown in sustainable forests.

10 9 8 7 6 5 4 3 2 1  (HB)
10 9 8 7 6 5 4 3 2 1  (PB)

# GRANNY CAME HERE ON THE EMPIRE WINDRUSH

PATRICE LAWRENCE

Illustrated by Camilla Sucre

 nosy crow

EMPIRE

Ava's granny was the best singer in the world. She was always teaching Ava old songs from Trinidad, the Caribbean island where she'd grown up. On Sundays, Ava and Granny sang together at the top of their voices. They even opened the windows so everyone outside could hear them too.

But today, Ava stopped halfway through their favourite song.
"What's wrong, honey?" Granny asked.
"I need to find a costume for school tomorrow," Ava said.
"We have to dress up as someone we admire. I've been thinking
about it all weekend, but I still don't know who I should be."
"Ah," Granny said. "Maybe I can help. Come with me."
Ava grinned. She knew exactly where they were going.
To the trunk!

The special trunk full of old clothes! The trunk where you
could dive inside and come out as someone completely different.
Granny lifted the heavy lid and rummaged inside.
At last, she held up a necklace of bright, sparkling beads.

"How about Winifred Atwell?" Granny said. "She was from
Trinidad, like me."
"Did she come on that Empire Windrush boat too, Granny?"

"No," Granny said. "Winifred came to England a few years before the Empire Windrush. She was a famous musician and played the piano like a dream. When those stage lights hit her jewels, they shone like the stars back home."

Ava stared at the necklace and tried to imagine it glowing around her neck like stars. She'd never heard of Winifred Atwell, though, so how could Ava know if she admired her?

"Can we try someone else, Granny?"

This time, they both leaned into the trunk and dug through the clothes.

Granny pulled out a red scarf.

"What about Mary Seacole? She's so important that there's a painting of her in a famous art gallery in London. And she's wearing a scarf just like this."

Ava had heard of Mary Seacole.

"She was a nurse," she said. "Just like Mummy and Daddy!"

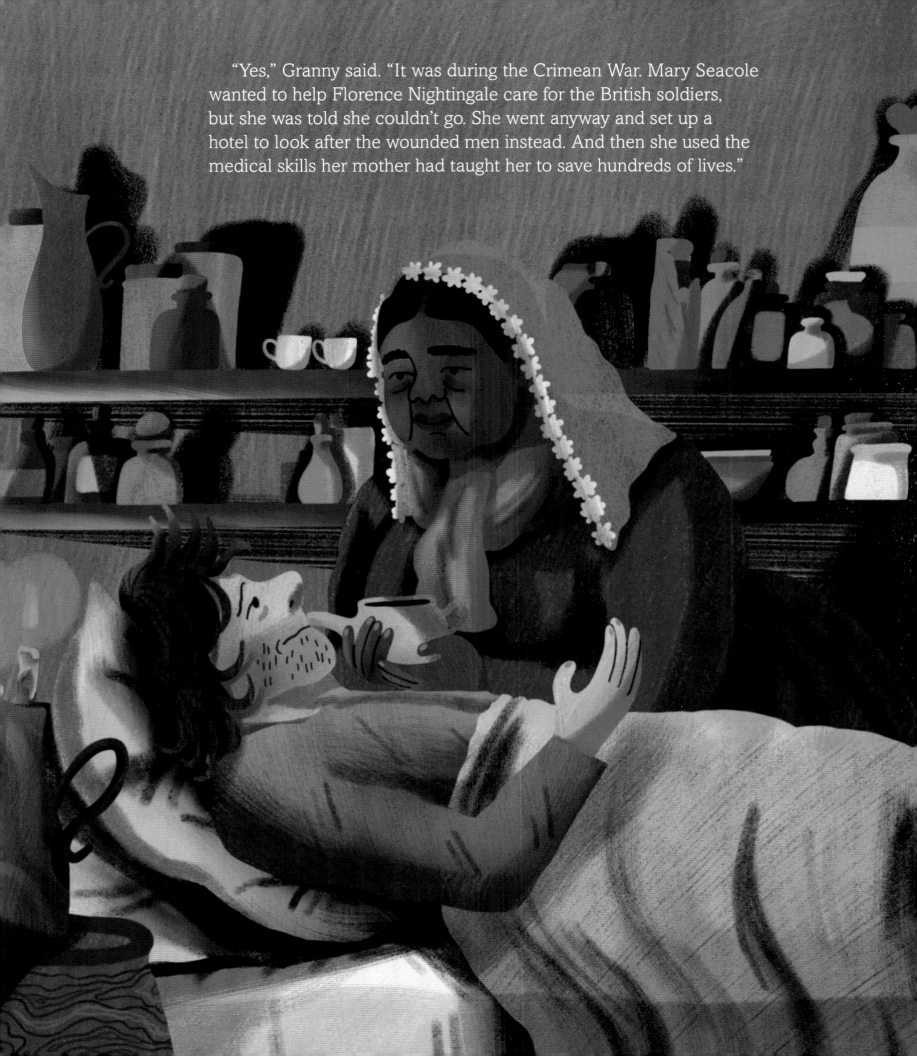

"Yes," Granny said. "It was during the Crimean War. Mary Seacole wanted to help Florence Nightingale care for the British soldiers, but she was told she couldn't go. She went anyway and set up a hotel to look after the wounded men instead. And then she used the medical skills her mother had taught her to save hundreds of lives."

Granny wound the scarf around Ava's neck. Ava did admire
Mary Seacole, but the only problem was that Ava's cousin, Amore,
admired her too.

"Sorry, Granny," Ava said. "I think Amore's dressing up as
Mary Seacole."

"OK, honey. Let's try again."

Ava and Granny both leaned so far into the trunk that Ava
thought they were going to fall right in.

Granny lifted out a jacket. It was a little wrinkly and much
too big for Ava.

"How about Rosa Parks?" Granny said. "You know her story,
don't you?"

"Yes," Ava said. "She wouldn't give up her seat on the bus for
a white person."

"Exactly so," Granny said. "In America, Black people were only allowed to sit in the seats at the back of buses. If a white person wanted their seat, the Black person had to give it up. Rosa Parks said 'no' and got arrested by the police. But in the end, Rosa helped change some very unfair laws."

Rosa Parks was one of Ava's heroes, but everyone in Ava's school had heard of her. Ava even knew that two of her best friends were planning to dress up as Rosa Parks.

Ava was getting ready to dive into the trunk again when she spotted a small suitcase at the bottom, hidden beneath the clothes. She'd never noticed it before.

"What's this, Granny?" she asked.

Granny lifted it out and carefully laid it on the bed.

"This was my grip," she said. "I brought it from Trinidad with me on the Empire Windrush."

Ava ran her hand across the suitcase. "It's made of cardboard!"

"Yes," Granny laughed. "I wish I knew who first thought it was a good idea to carry a cardboard case to rainy England!"

"Can we look inside?"

"Of course, honey."

Granny clicked the catches, first the right one,
then the left, and Ava opened the case wide.
"Everything in here was given to me as a present,"
Granny said.
A present? Ava thought that these were
very strange presents.

An empty jar.

A smooth grey pebble.

A little blue hat.

A pair of lace gloves.

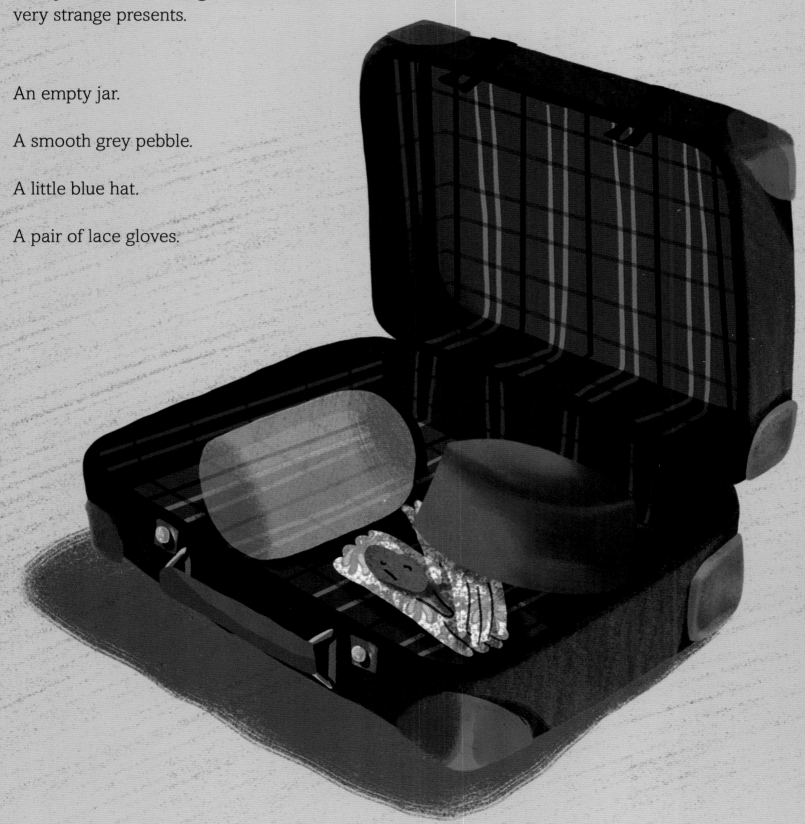

Ava shook the jar. It really was empty.

"Who gave you this, Granny?"

"That was my Tante Olive," Granny said. "Ma's sister. She knew I would be on that big, old boat for nearly a month before I reached England, so she filled a jar with dried orange peel to settle my stomach. When those waves rolled me from side to side, I opened this jar and breathed in the smell of oranges. Suddenly, it was like I was back in Tante's yard, laughing with my cousins."

EMPIRI
LO

Ava picked up the pebble and let it rest in the palm of her hand.
"And this, Granny?"
"A present from my little sister, Marva. It was my birthday the day
before I left Trinidad and we went bathing in the river. Marva wanted
me to think about her every time I swam in the Thames. When we
finally docked at Tilbury and I saw that cold, smelly river jammed
with boats, I knew that I would never be bathing in there!"

The blue hat must have been much too small for Granny.
It wouldn't even fit on Ava's head.
"Was this really yours?" Ava asked.
Granny laughed.
"My cousin Maureen was the same age as you are now.
She made it especially for me to keep my head warm in England.
I used to think of her little fingers sewing it when I went to work
in the clothes factory. Every day, it was the thud, thud, thud of
the sewing machines in my ears. It made me want to march
across land and sea back to Trinidad.

Even so, in some ways, I was lucky," Granny said. "At least I had a place to stay. Some men I knew were turned away from lodgings, again and again, just because they were Black."

Ava slipped on one of the lace gloves. She wiggled her fingers around inside.

"These were from Ma," Granny sighed. "I was to save them for when I had tea with the Queen."

"You met the Queen, Granny?"

"No, honey, I didn't meet the Queen, but I did meet someone very special. In those first few months, I struggled so hard. Autumn came and all the trees died. I thought they would never wake up again. The cold wrapped itself around me and wouldn't let go.

I missed my family and the sunshine and the mangoes warm from
Tante Olive's tree. I missed the fireflies and the hummingbirds
and the mountains glowing orange with immortelle blossom.

I just wanted to go home."

"But you stayed, Granny," Ava said.

"Yes," Granny said. "I stayed. Even when the clouds lay heavy, sunshine can still break through.

I met your grandad. He was the conductor on the bus that took me to work every day. At first, we would just smile at each other. Then it was 'good morning'. Soon, in spite of the noise in the factory, I looked forward to my morning journey." Granny smiled. "And my journeys home, when he would cross the whole of London just to come and meet me."

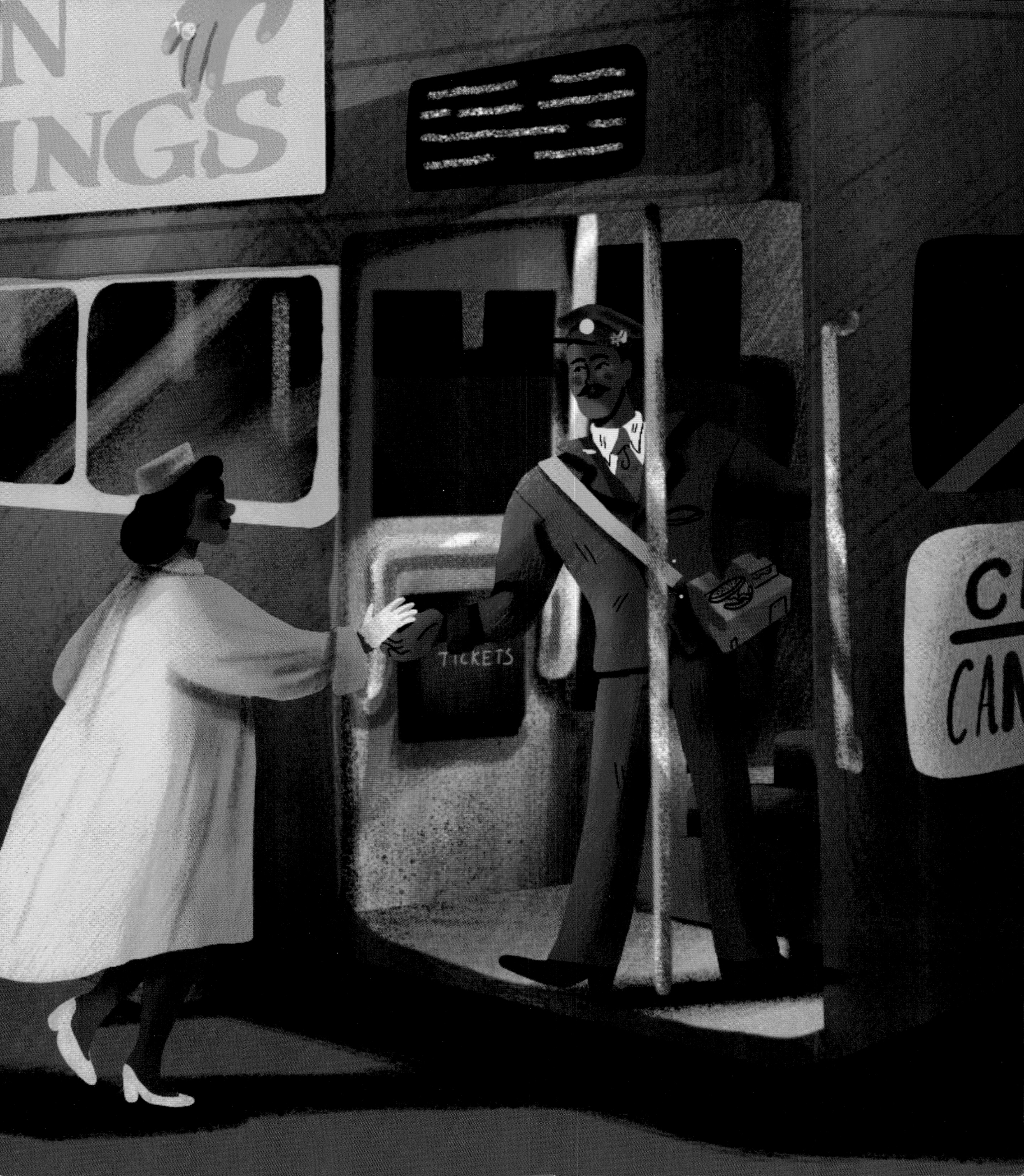
TICKETS

Granny wriggled her own hand into the other lace glove.

"After winter, spring came again," she said. "The rain stopped and the sun was shining and the clouds lifted so high, I could see the gold all around me."

"Real gold, Granny?"

"Even better than real gold. Some people are more precious than all the gold in the world."

"So have you decided, Ava?" Granny asked. "Will it be Winifred or Mary or Rosa?"

"I have decided," Ava said. "But it's not going to be any of them. I'm going to dress up as someone I admire even more."

"Oh my," Granny said. "They must be really special."

"She is," Ava said . . .

"It's someone who came to England on her own on a big, old boat called the Empire Windrush. Someone who was cold and sad and wanted to go back to the sunshine and her family in Trinidad. Someone who stayed and sings and makes me and everyone happy . . .

. . . Someone who is more precious than all the gold in the world.

My granny!"